MAC & CHEESE

James Proimos

Christy Ottaviano Books

HENRY HOLT AND COMPANY · NEW YORK

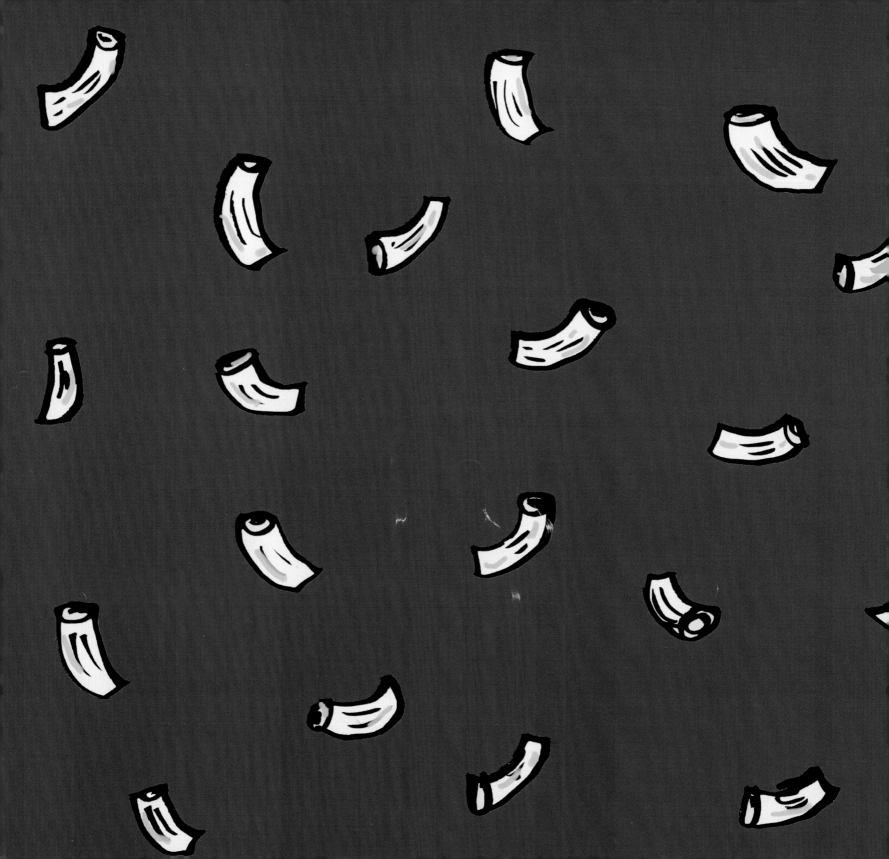

After a lovely breakfast, Mac and Cheese went on a long walk.

"Mac, you are the smartest noodle I know," said Cheese.

"I can't argue with that, Cheese," said Mac.

"There's probably nothing you don't know, is there, Mac?" asked Cheese.

"There is no probably about it,"

answered Mac.

"What is one plus one, Mac?" asked Cheese.

"That's too easy."

"Please tell me," begged Cheese.

"One plus one equals two," said Mac.

"Holy moly!"

yelled Cheese.

"I'm greatly impressed."

"Mac, I have another question," said Cheese.

"Ready when you are," said Mac.

"What is the second letter of the alphabet? Tricky, right?" asked Cheese.

"That's not tricky at all, Cheese. The second letter of the alphabet is B!" answered Mac.

"Moly Holy!" yelled Cheese.

"You have a big, big brain."

Cheese thought long and hard about his next question. Finally, it came to him.

"Mac, what is two plus B?" asked Cheese.

Mac blinked seven times.

"I don't think I heard you correctly, Cheese," said Mac. "Could you repeat the question?"

"What is two plus B?"

Mac thought long and hard about this question. Even longer and harder than it had taken Cheese to come up with the question.

In fact, he thought so hard it looked like he might hurt himself.

"Don't worry about it, Mac. It was a silly question," said Cheese.

"No, no, I almost have it figured out," said Mac.

"That's all well and good, but I have a much better question," said Cheese. "Are there any two friends who belong together more than we do?"

"Of course there are no two friends who belong together more than we do!" answered Mac.

"Even I knew that one," laughed Cheese.

"I knew you knew," said Mac.

Just then, Mac noticed two jars playing catch in the field.

"Hey, look— it's P.B. and Jay!"

said Cheese.

"Oh no, not them!" said Mac.

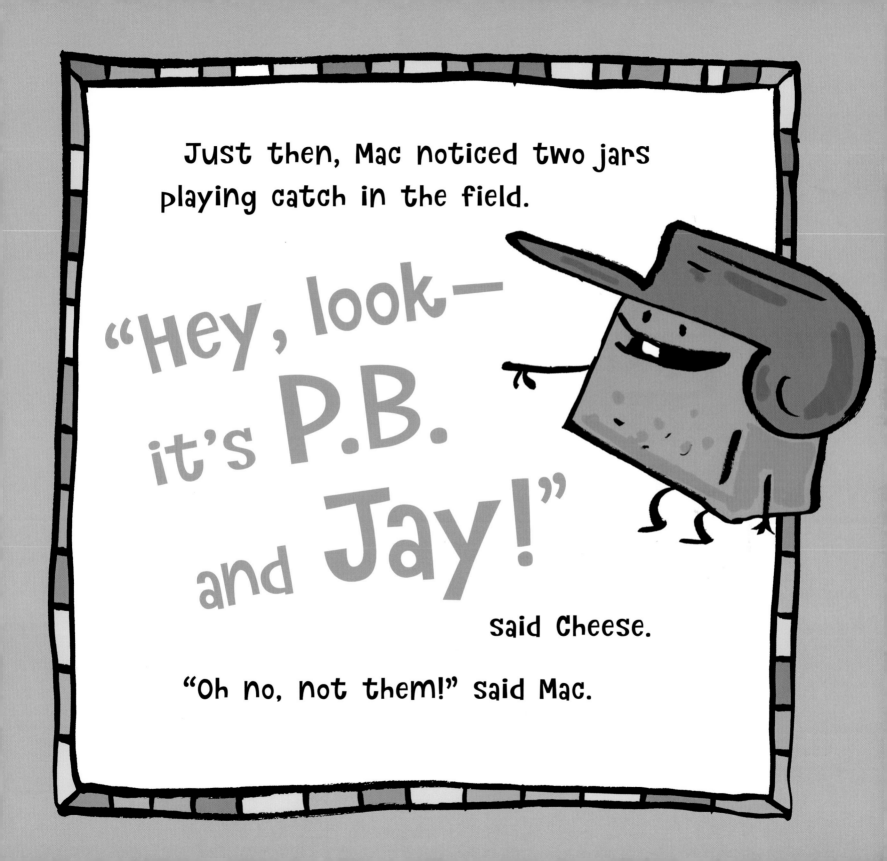

After a light lunch, Cheese decided to create a large painting. When Mac walked into the room, he was very confused.

"What on earth is that?"

asked Mac.

"It's an orange, of course," answered Cheese.

"But it's blue! Oranges are orange."

"Not in my painting,"

said Cheese.

"Follow me to my kitchen," said Cheese.

Mac followed Cheese.

"Check out this picture of an orange that I taped to my refrigerator," said Cheese. "You're going to love it."

"This is all wrong," said Mac.

"It's the color orange, is it not?" asked Cheese.

"Yes, it is orange. But it's a triangle," said Mac. "Oranges are round!"

"Not in my painting," said Cheese.

"Follow me to my dining room," said Cheese.

Mac followed Cheese.

"Check out this picture of an orange that I hung over the fireplace," said Cheese.

"That's just a painting of you, Cheese!"

"It is me, Mac. After I ate an orange! It's in my tummy!"

"In your tummy? I'm outraged!" said Mac.

"Sometimes art should be outrageous," said Cheese.

"That is the worst picture of an orange I have ever seen," said Mac.

Just then, Salt and Salt showed up and said in unison, "That is awful."

"Mac, this is not another picture of an orange," said Cheese. "It is a picture of my best friend."

"ME?" asked Mac. "Oh my. Am I the big red blob?"

"No, Mac. You are the yellow smudge. Because you are the brightest of all."

"Now we see," said Salt and Salt. "We like it."

"Do you like it, Mac?" asked Cheese.

"It is a masterpiece, Cheese. You are a great artist."

"That makes me so happy, Mac, because you are always right," said Cheese.

"Well, not always. I may have been wrong about your paintings of oranges."

"Oh boy!" yelled Cheese.

"I said I MAY have been wrong," said Mac.

"Still. Oh boy!" yelled a very happy Cheese.

After dinner, Mac and Cheese went for a long walk.

"What a beautiful night," said Cheese.

"Look, the Big Dipper!"

Said Mac.

"Fantastic!" said Cheese.

"You may want to paint that," said Mac.

"I just might," said Cheese.

Mac and Cheese walked a bit farther.

"Do you hear that?" said Mac.

Cheese listened hard.

"I don't hear a thing," said Cheese.

"Exactly. Isn't it beautiful?"

"Yes," said Cheese.
"It is."

But suddenly, a loud commotion broke the beautiful silence.

It was Oil and Water. They were arguing about the weather.

Oil was yelling that it was going to rain. Water was yelling that it was not going to do anything of the sort.

"Sheesh!"

said Cheese after Oil and Water passed by.

"On that note, let's call it a day," said Mac.

And that's what they did.

That night, Cheese dreamed of numbers and letters.

Eventually, he was dreaming only of Zs.

It reminded him of his friend Mac.

That made him happy.

And he slept very well.

· - Z Z z - ·

That night, Mac dreamed of purple broccoli.

Mac knew broccoli was usually green, but he liked it because purple broccoli reminded him of his friend Cheese.

That made him happy.

And he slept very well too.

For James Marshall and Arnold Lobel

Henry Holt and Company, LLC, *Publishers since 1866*
175 Fifth Avenue, New York, New York 10010
mackids.com

Library of Congress Cataloging-in-Publication Data
Names: Proimos, James, author, illustrator.
Title: Mac & Cheese / James Proimos.
Description: First Edition. | New York : Henry Holt and Company 2016. | Summary: "Best friends
Mac and Cheese prove that it is important to always be yourself"— Provided by publisher.
Identifiers: LCCN 2015038620 | ISBN 9780805091564 (hardback)
Subjects: | CYAC: Best friends—Fiction. | Individuality—Fiction. | BISAC: JUVENILE FICTION /
Social Issues / Friendship. | JUVENILE FICTION / Humorous Stories.
Classification: LCC PZ7.P9432 Mac 2016 | DDC [E]—dc23
LC record available at https://lccn.loc.gov/2015038620

Our books may be purchased in bulk for promotional, educational, or business use.
Please contact your local bookseller or the Macmillan Corporate and Premium Sales Department
at (800) 221-7945 ext. 5442 or by e-mail at MacmillanSpecialMarkets@macmillan.com.

First Edition—2016 / Designed by April Ward and Becca Syracuse
The artist used brush pen on paper and colored in Sketchbook Pro to create the illustrations for this book.

Printed in China by RR Donnelley Asia Printing Solutions Ltd., Dongguan City, Guangdong Province
1 3 5 7 9 10 8 6 4 2